Loud Mouth

Other Orchard Storybooks

A WOODSIDE SCHOOL STORY

Loud Mouth

JEAN URE

Illustrated by
LYNNE WILLEY

ORCHARD BOOKS
London

To Julia, who helps me
with my sums

Text copyright © Jean Ure 1988
Illustrations copyright © LYNNE WILLEY 1988
First published in Great Britain in 1988 by
ORCHARD BOOKS
10 Golden Square, London W1R 3AF
Orchard Books Australia
14 Mars Road, Lane Cove NSW 2066
Orchard Books Canada
20 Torbay Road, Markham, Ontario 23P 1G6
1 85213 086 5
Printed in Great Britain

Chapter 1

Everbody was just about sick of Leonie Shanks.

"Great stupid show-off," said Alison Webb. She did a little twirl, being Leonie showing off. "Look at my new *dress*, look at my new *shoes*—"

"Look at my new *pencil* case—"

"Look at my new *hair*—"

"Makes you sick," grumbled Shirin Shah. Shirin was Alison's best friend and the prettiest girl in the class. She couldn't stand Leonie Shanks. Leonie Loud Mouth was what Shirin called her.

Nobody could stand Leonie. Even

Pavindra, who never had a bad word to say for anyone, couldn't actually think of anything *good*. All Pavindra could think of was, "Her things that she has are very nice things."

"Yeah—that's why she shows 'em off!" Jackie-Lee Gibbs bounced her netball on the ground and kicked at it, hard, with the toe of her wellie. The netball sailed across the playground and out through the school gate. On its way out, it bumped into something on its way in. The something was a bright red, brand new bicycle. Riding it was Leonie Shanks.

Leonie wobbled dangerously as the netball banged into her. The netball bounced off the front wheel and rolled into the kerb. Leonie just about managed to keep upright.

"Watch my new bike!" screamed Leonie.

"Give it a kick," said Shirin, as Jackie went after her netball.

Jackie couldn't kick the bike because Leonie's mother was standing outside the gate watching Leonie go in. She smiled at Jackie, which meant that Jackie had to smile back.

"Leonie's come to school on her new bicycle," said Mrs Shanks.

"Oh, is that what it is? I thought it was a camel."

(That was what Jackie *said* that she had said, when she was telling the others, afterwards, but of course it wasn't really. Really she wouldn't have dared.)

As she ran back with her netball she found Leonie already showing off her new possession, riding it in circles round the group from Class 5.

"Can I have a go?" begged Sophie Waters. Sophie was always so *eager*. Jackie wouldn't have lowered herself.

9

Leonie hesitated. She cast a glance over her shoulder at her mother, still beaming and nodding at the school gate.

"No," she said. "I don't think you'd better. You might bash it into something."

Sophie grew pink. "I wouldn't! I promise! I know how to ride a bicycle."

"Yes, but this is *new*," said Leonie. She stopped and dismounted. "It was very expensive. It's one of the best sort of bikes you can buy."

"Looks like a perfectly ordinary sort of bike to me," scoffed Jackie.

"How would you know?" said Leonie. "You haven't got one."

"Charming!" Shirin sniffed, and linked her arm through Spider's. (Spider was Alison's nickname, because of being called Webb.) "Let's go and talk to someone that has better manners." She looked at Jackie. "You coming?"

Jackie was torn. In spite of what she'd said about the bicycle, Leonie was quite right: it *was* a good one. Jackie would have given a lot to have a bicycle like that.

"Suit yourself," said Shirin.

Shirin didn't have a lot of patience. She stalked off across the playground with Spider, followed after a second or so by the rest of the group. Only Jackie was left, and Pavindra.

"I'm going to put my bicycle away now," said Leonie. She wheeled it over to the cycle rack. There was one other bicycle in the rack and that was Miss Lilly's. All the rest of the teachers came by bus or by car. "I've got a special padlock for it. It's got a secret combination, like a safe. You have to click it round till you get the right numbers." Leonie stood there, self-importantly clicking. "I mustn't tell anyone what the numbers are," she said, "because then they could

12

open the padlock and steal the bike."

"Suppose you forgot them?" said Jackie.

"I can't forget them. I've got a special secret way of how to remember." Triumphantly, Leonie pulled open her padlock and snapped it shut again round the front wheel of the bike. "Do you want to know what it is?"

"Not particularly," said Jackie, though of course she did.

"It's ever so easy," said Leonie. "All I do, I just say FIDO... and then I remember. Clever, isn't it? 'Cos I'm the only one that knows what it means. *You* could say FIDO as much as you like and the bike wouldn't move. But if *I* say it—"

"Say it," said Jackie.

"Not now," said Leonie. "I've put it away now. And anyway, that was the bell... hey, Soozie!" Leonie went chasing off across the playground after Soozie Schuster. "Have you seen my new bicycle? It was ever so expensive. It's one of the best kind of bikes—"

"Show-off," said Jackie. She gave one last cross look at the new bicycle. "I don't see how just saying FIDO can make a padlock open."

"It's the letters," said Pavindra. "You have to turn them into numbers."

Jackie wrinkled her forehead. "How?"

15

"You have to work it, with the alphabet...a, b, c, until you get to F. Then I. Then—"

"Like a code." Jackie bounced her netball. "Stupid loud mouth! Now she's gone and told us."

Chapter 2

Leonie really was quite obnoxious about her new bicyle. She hadn't done as much show-ing off as this since the beginning of term, when she had come to school wearing the new ear muffs and leg warmers that she had had for Christmas.

She had gone round boasting that the ear muffs were made out of real mink. It had served her jolly well right when Catherine Onslow had turned on her. Everyone had been really surprised, because Catherine was usually such a mouse. She had told Leonie that people who wore animal fur were hateful and loathsome and that she was never going to talk to her ever again.

This had made Soozie Schuster say that she was never going to talk to her ever again, either, and then Sophie Waters had said neither was she. In the end all the class had ganged up against her, until she had been forced to admit that the ear muffs weren't really mink at all, but only imitation.

During morning break was when Leonie was worst at her showing off. She kept going up to people—people who were quite happily doing their own thing, minding their own business—and saying, "Have you seen my new bicycle?"

"As if anybody *wants* to see the stupid thing!"

Shirin in particular found Leonie an annoyance. What she specially found annoying was the way Leonie kept curling strands of long blonde hair about her fingers as she talked.

Shirin's hair was long and black, but she couldn't curl it round her fingers because when they were at school they had to wear their hair in plaits and Shirin didn't have lots of fuzzy loose strands as Leonie did. Leonie's strands sprung out like corkscrews all round her face. When she pulled them out straight they were several centimetres long.

"*I* think," said Shirin, "that it's about time we did something."

"What sort of something?"

"Something to *stop* her."

"Stop her talking?"

"Stop her showing off."

They thought about it.

"How?" said Sophie.

"We could have a society...an I Hate Leonie Shanks Society."

"What'd it do?"

"Hate Leonie Shanks!"

"But what'd it *do*?"

"Not speak to her. Not until she stopped showing off."

"Let's vote," said Spider. "Hands up everyone who thinks it's a good idea."

Those who put their hands up were: Spider, Shirin, Colette Goodchild, Sophie Waters, Suzanne Schuster, Claire Paddon, Sandra Martin and Kelly Flanagan. (They hadn't bothered with the boys, because mostly the boys took no notice of Leonie Shanks anyway.)

"Now hands up everyone who *doesn't* think it's a good idea."

The only two who didn't think it was a good idea were Catherine Onslow and Pavindra Patel. Nobody had expected Pavindra to vote for a hate society, but they had expected Catherine to. As Shirin pointed out, *she* was the one who had originally threatened to stop speaking, because of the mink ear muffs.

"That was different," said Catherine. "That was when I thought she was being cruel to animals."

"*I* vote," said Spider, "that anyone that talks to her from now on is sent to Coventry. That means," she added, for the benefit of people who mightn't know, such as Sandra Martin, who was thick, "that that person doesn't get talked to either."

Catherine bit her lip. It was only recently, since making friends with Soozie Schuster, that she had come out of her shell. Jackie could tell that this was really making her unhappy. After a struggle, Catherine said all right, she would agree not to talk so long as it was only for a short time—"Like just for one day."

"One day's no good!"

"Need to do it for at least a week."

"At *least*."

"Let's vote, let's vote!" Spider waved her arm in the air. "Hands up all those who agree that this is going to be **I Hate Leonie Shanks Week** and that from now till Friday evening no one is allowed to talk to her."

This time every hand went up, including Pavindra's. Catherine's went up reluctantly, but it did go up in the end.

"Right," said Shirin. "That's it. *Now* she'll jolly well learn!"

As they went out into the playground at dinner time Leonie said, "I'm going to go and look at my new bike. Who wants to come and watch?"

Silence. Nobody said a word.

"I expect I shall take the padlock off," said Leonie. "Probably."

More silence. Catherine looked uncomfortable, but she didn't say anything.

"Let's go and see if our bulbs are growing yet," said Spider.

They ran off, in a bunch, to look at the bulbs. Nobody was going to talk to Leonie Shanks for a whole week.

Chapter 3

"I hope you're taking good care of your new bicycle," said Leonie's mother, as she and Leonie were having tea together after school that day.

"Yes," said Leonie.

"It was very expensive, you know. Daddy had to pay a lot for that bicycle."

"Yes," said Leonie. "I know."

"We only want you to have the best. We could have got a cheaper one, but we didn't think you'd like it as much."

"No," said Leonie. She took a slice of carrot cake.

"What did the other girls think? Did they like it?"

"I suppose so," said Leonie.

"Only suppose so?"

Leonie chewed on her carrot cake.

"What did they say?"

"Said they liked it."

"Well, there you are, then!"

There was a silence. Leonie remembered that other silence: the silence at dinner time when none of them had spoken to her.

"Jackie Gibbs said it looked just like any ordinary sort of bike to her."

"Well, you can tell Jackie Gibbs that it most certainly isn't any ordinary sort of bike!"

"I told her."

"And she didn't believe you?"

Slowly, Leonie shook her head.

"I shouldn't take any notice, if I were you. She's probably just jealous."

That was it, thought Leonie; Jackie was jealous. They were all jealous, because of her having nice things and them not. It was good to have nice things, but it wasn't much fun if people were going to get all horrid and twisted about it. She would almost rather not have them if that was what it did to people.

"P'raps I oughtn't to use my bicycle for going to school on?" she said.

"Nonsense! Of course you must use it— that's what we bought it for. You mustn't let some jealous little girl put you off. We can't all have everything we want. That's a lesson we soon have to learn."

"But it might get messed up ... if it rains,

or something."

"Don't worry! I wouldn't let you use it if it rained. The roads might be slippy."

That night, Leonie prayed that it would rain. Of course, it didn't. It rained all the time when you didn't want it to, like on sports days or picnics; but never when you did.

Her mother came as far as the school gate with her. Leonie wished that she wouldn't.

"Just for another day or two, until I'm absolutely certain that you're safe," said her mother.

She was as safe as could be. All she had to do was cycle along the footpath by the side of the woods and there she was, in Woodside Glade, directly opposite school.

"Which is the little girl who's jealous?" said Mrs Shanks.

Leonie cringed. "I don't think she's here."

Jackie *was* there. She was racing round the playground with her netball, with Diane Evans and Kelly Flanagan.

"That's a pity," said Mrs Shanks. "I'd have had a word with her. All right! Off you go. I'll just stay and see you put your bike away."

Leonie dismounted and wheeled her bicycle across the playground. She wished her mother would go. Other mothers didn't stand around watching.

Miss Lilly was at the cycle rack, unstrapping her briefcase.

"Good morning, Leonie," she said. "That's a very splendid machine you have there!"

Leonie smiled, gratefully. At least Miss Lilly appreciated her new bicycle. Miss Lilly wasn't jealous.

Leonie padlocked the front wheel and picked up her school bag. Nearby, Sandra Martin and Claire Paddon were frightening themselves with a black rubber snake, throwing it at each other and screeching if it came too close.

"I've got one of those," said Leonie. "Only mine's bigger than that...I should think mine's probably a *python*."

Screech! went Claire, as the snake hit her in the face. Shriek! went Sandra, as Claire lobbed it back. They took absolutely no notice of Leonie at all.

"You can get them at that stall," said Leonie. "Down the market. They've got hundreds of them . . . snakes and frogs and lizardy things . . . I've got a big furry spider. It's *huge*. It looks just like a real one. It cost ever such a lot."

Claire and Sandra went on ignoring her.

"All right," said Leonie. "Play with your silly old snake . . . it didn't cost half as much as my spider!"

Over in the corner, Pavindra was standing by herself. She decided that she would go and talk to Pavindra.

"I've got a big spider at home. *And* a snake. If I brought them in, we could play with them."

Pavindra gave her a scared look and didn't say anything.

"Shall I?" said Leonie. "My snake's much better than their one."

Pavindra looked as if she might be going to cry. Still she didn't say anything. Maybe she was just scared of snakes and spiders.

The bell rang and they went into school. One of the boys said, "Har, har, Leonie Sheepshanks," and some of them sniggered,

because that was their idea of a joke. None of the girls said anything.

Nobody said anything to Leonie all through the morning (not unless they absolutely had to, for class). At dinner time, when she sat down next to Soozie Schuster, Soozie began sniffing the air and said, "Pooh! I smell something nasty," and edged her chair away. Soon the whole table was sniffing the air and saying that they could

smell something nasty, too.

Leonie hated them. They were all jealous; they were all horrible.

Not only were they all jealous and horrible, but Jackie-Lee Gibbs was a *thief* . . .

Chapter 4

Of course, Jackie knew that she oughtn't to have tried unlocking the padlock on Leonie's bicycle. She hadn't meant to. She had gone after her netball, which had rolled down near the cycle racks. She'd stood there a moment, just looking at the bike and thinking about the padlock and about what Pavindra had said. "It's the letters . . . you have to turn them into numbers."

FIDO . . . . .

She had gone through the alphabet on her fingers. F was 6, I was 9, D was 4, O was—what was O? O must be nought. Six-nine-four-nought . . .

Jackie had bent down to examine the padlock. Somehow, before she knew it, she had been turning it, clicking it, watching the little numbers come up. She had just got as far as 694 when Leonie had appeared.

"What are you doing with my bicycle?" Leonie had shrilled. "Leave it alone, you're not to touch it, it's mine!"

And then Leonie had seen that her special secret padlock was almost undone, and she had started jumping and screaming and accusing Jackie of all kinds of terrible things.

"You're a thief, you're a thief! You're trying to steal my bicycle! You're jealous!"

Jackie had been so indignant that she had been stung into retaliating: "Who'd be jealous of you, stupid Sheepshanks? Nobody'll even talk to you no more 'cos you're such a show-off!"

Too late, she realised: she had broken her

vow of silence. If Spider and Shirin knew they would be furious with her. They would probably impose some fearful punishment, like making her walk along the top of the wall by the lavatories. Cameron Philips had once fallen off that wall and busted his arm.

"I could tell Miss Lilly about you!" Leonie had shrieked; but Jackie had snatched up her netball and run.

She had spent the rest of the day expecting Miss Lilly to say, "Jackie, I'd like a word with you," but the day passed and Miss Lilly didn't say anything. Maybe Leonie had thought better of it.

That afternoon, as they were in the cloakroom putting on their coats ready to go home, there was a sudden loud scream from the far end, where Leonie had her peg. Miss Lilly came running.

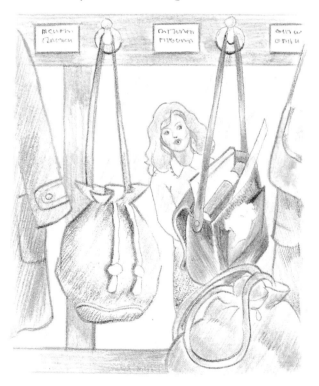

"Good heavens, Leonie! Whatever is the matter?"

"My ear muffs!" screeched Leonie. "Somebody's taken my ear muffs!"

"Are you absolutely certain," said Miss Lilly, "that you were wearing your ear muffs?"

"I suppose it was the *mink* ones?" said Shirin.

"Mink?" said Miss Lilly. She sounded alarmed.

"They weren't really mink," said Catherine. "Only pretend."

"Oh! That's a relief. Still, we must try to find them. Where did you put them when you got to school, Leonie?"

Leonie, between sobs and hiccups, said that she had hung them over her peg.

"Does anybody remember seeing them?" said Miss Lilly, but nobody did.

They discussed it, afterwards, when Leonie had gone sobbing off with Miss Lilly to report the missing ear muffs to Mrs Kenny, in the Office. Everyone was of the opinion that it would jolly well serve her right if someone *had* pinched the stupid things. They had all had more than enough of Leonie and her ear muffs.

"These are my new *ear* muffs, that were given to me at *Christmas*." Spider made a being-sick noise. "*Yuck.*"

"Pity someone doesn't take My New Bicycle," said Shirin. "That'd give her something to think about."

Jackie felt her cheeks grow hot. How awful, if anyone ever did take the new bicycle! Leonie would be bound to say that it was her.

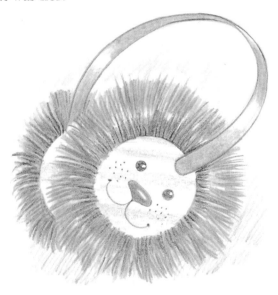

Chapter 5

Next morning on her way in to school, Jackie saw Leonie ahead of her, further down the road. Leonie was just leaving home on her bicycle. Her mother was at the gate, waving her goodbye. Jackie heard her voice, calling out: "Make sure you go straight there!"

She watched as Leonie pedalled off, along the pavement. She saw her bump down the kerb and wobble across the grass before turning into the footpath by the side of the woods.

By the time Jackie reached the footpath, Leonie had completely disappeared. She must have pedalled like mad to have got to the other end of the path before Jackie arrived. As a matter of fact, Jackie didn't understand how she could have done it. The footpath was a long one, and Jackie hadn't been *that* far behind.

She looked down, and saw the tyre marks where the bicycle had gone. The ground along the footpath was always soft and squidgy, except in summer, when it went to dust. Jackie amused herself by treading exactly the same track as Leonie, squashing the tyre marks beneath her wellies.

Suddenly, about half way down, the tyre marks stopped. That was odd! Where had they gone?

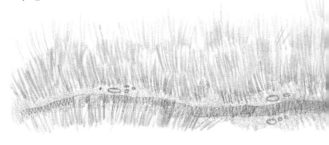

Jackie squatted down to examine the ground more closely. She discovered that the marks hadn't actually stopped, they had simply become fainter and had changed direction: instead of going straight on down the path they had turned at right angles, into the woods.

The fact that the marks were fainter must mean that Leonie had dismounted and started wheeling instead of riding—which of course she would have to do if she were going into the woods. The undergrowth was far too thick for riding. But whatever had she gone there for? Jackie was sure Mrs Shanks wouldn't approve. Even Jackie's mother, who wasn't given to fussing, told Jackie that she was always to keep to the footpath.

Maybe Leonie had been *kidnapped*?

Jackie stood quite still, and listened. She couldn't hear anything, except the far-off

rumble of traffic on the main road and the sound of birdsong in the woods.

She looked again at the entrance where Leonie had wheeled her bike. There was a sort of path there. Not one of the proper paths, where people went walking; more like a secret way that someone had made. Jackie could see, when she looked carefully, where the bicycle had been wheeled.

Cautiously, ready to turn and run at any moment, she stepped into the woods and set off on the trail of Leonie and her bicycle.

She hadn't gone very far when she heard it: a strange scritching sound, as if someone were ripping a piece of material.

Jackie froze. That was what people did that kidnapped you. They ripped all your clothes off and left them lying around under bushes for the police to find later.

Jackie turned. She was about to go pelting off, back to Mrs Shanks's house to get help, when she heard something else. This time it wasn't a scritching sound. It was the sound of a voice.

It was Leonie's voice.

"...pulled me off my bike," it was saying, "so that I fell over in the mud."

She didn't sound at all frightened; not at all like you would expect a person to sound that was being kidnapped.

Jackie crept forward again, through the undergrowth. She came to a nest of holly bushes with just enough of an opening for someone fairly small to crawl through. She put her head down and crawled.

The holly bushes grew in a circle. Inside the circle was a little den. Inside the little den was Leonie. She was rubbing mud over herself.

Jackie stood watching, too surprised to speak. Leonie didn't see her at first. She just went on rubbing mud, up and down, on her pale blue anorak which had been new last term. "My new anorak...see! It's quilted." Now it was covered in mud and had a large jagged hole torn in it.

Leonie suddenly looked up and saw Jackie. Her eyes went huge and staring, her cheeks grew bright scarlet.

"Someone knocked me off my bicycle,"she babbled. "They knocked me off my bicycle and I fell in the mud, and I don't know who it was because I couldn't see them, they came up behind and knocked me off, and they stole my bike and—"

Jackie's gaze moved slowly from the spectacle of Leonie, smeared with mud, in her ragged anorak, to a pair of gleaming handlebars, sticking out of a holly bush. Leonie's gaze followed Jackie's. There was a long silence.

"I s'pose you were going to say it was me that took it?"

"No," whispered Leonie.

Jackie walked across and pulled the bicycle into the open. On the ground, tucked away behind the bicycle, was a plastic bag. Inside the plastic bag was a pair of ear muffs.

"Are you going to tell?" whispered Leonie.

"What d'you take me for?" said Jackie. "I'm not a sneak!"

It would make a jolly good story, Leonie Shanks going and stealing her own things; but for all that she wouldn't tell. Leonie hadn't told about her and the padlock.

"You'd better wipe that mud off," she said.

Leonie stood, helpless, while Jackie did the best she could with some paper hankies.

"It's not very good," said Jackie. "You'll have to say you fell off."

Leonie nodded, dumbly.

"Here—" Jackie held out the plastic bag. "You can always tell Miss you made a mistake ... say you found them at home."

Leonie backed away.

"I don't want them! You have them."

Jackie was tempted. She'd often envied

Leonie her nice things.

"Best not," she said. "But I wouldn't mind a ride on your bike."

At the school gate, they bumped into Shirin. Shirin looked at Jackie as if she could hardly believe her eyes.

"She fell off." Jackie jerked her thumb at Leonie. "We're just going to go and get her cleaned up. Later on, if they want, people can have a ride on her bike. Isn't that right?" She turned to Leonie. "People can have a go on your bike?"

"Yes," said Leonie.

Shirin didn't say anything; just narrowed her eyes and stalked away.

The word was soon out: anyone having a go on Leonie Shanks's bike would be sent to Coventry . . .

Catherine was the first to have a go, and then Suzanne, and then Kelly Flanagan, who didn't know how, so Leonie offered to teach her.

During the dinner break, Sandra Martin and Claire Paddon wanted to try, and then Sophie Waters couldn't resist it, which meant that Colette Goodchild couldn't, either.

They were all sent to Coventry.

By the end of the day, the only two people who hadn't been sent there were Spider and Shirin. They were still talking to each other, but they weren't talking to anybody else.

"Makes a nice change," said Jackie, doing wheelies on Class 5's bike, "not having them two bossing us around..."